DRAGON COINS

CONNOR WHITELEY

No part of this book may be reproduced in any form or by any electronic or mechanical means. Including information storage, and retrieval systems, without written permission from the author except for the use of brief quotations in a book review.

This book is NOT legal, professional, medical, financial or any type of official advice.

Any questions about the book, rights licensing, or to contact the author, please email connorwhiteley@connorwhiteley.net

Copyright © 2022 CONNOR WHITELEY

All rights reserved.

DEDICATION
Thank you to all my readers without you I couldn't do what I love.

DRAGON COINS

As Cato stepped into the Dragon Bar, he was instantly hit with the delicious fruity smells of the food. Hints of sweet fruits and desserts filled his senses. And encouraged him to go deeper into the Bar.

Cato always thought this place was a little weird because it was far from the Bar that common people went to every night. Instead, as Cato walked through the Bar, he passed high end large glass tables with people elegantly crowded around them. Wearing posh and expensive clothes and jewellery. Although, he did have to admit this so-called posh place didn't feel right. It felt strange.

Scanning the Bar, Cato tried to see the faces of these people but everyone was dressed in their own stunning posh clothes and they were packed too tightly together for their faces to be clear from a distance. And their constant loud talking was a distraction.

A part of Cato wondered why his sister wanted to come here. He knew this place only from a single memory but it was… impressionable. Since this was the first time each of them had picked up a man. Cato smiled at the thought. That was a pleasant night.

But it still didn't explain why his sister, a princess, wanted to come here. Especially, with them not seeing each other for over 5 or 6 years.

His skin started to feel warm as Cato walked over the edge of the Bar. From here he could see all the tables, chatting posh guests and the rather attractive waiters bringing the food out. Now, he thought about it. It might have been a waiter he picked up that night.

Regardless of that memory, all Cato wanted was to see his sister. He wanted to catch up with her. What had she been doing lately? Was she married?

The last question made Cato pause. The last he had heard his sister had been doing something in the delivery service. Making sure the delivery dragons throughout the Realm weren't being used by criminals. And there was a rumour about her dating a Baron. But who knows by now?

Cato lent on the brown cold hard wooden wall to try and blend in a little more. But his back and stomach pulsed with immense pain from old injuries.

He knew he shouldn't have come here before he was healed. After all he had almost died burning down that fanatical Church. He should have healed first. Yet Cato had to see his sister.

A hand touched his arm carefully making Cato turn round to see a young woman cloaked in an elegant metallic blue robe.

The woman rose her head slightly to reveal a massive smile and her majestic youthful features and the robe only amplified her dark blue eyes.

Cato beamed a little and turned away so it might look like they didn't know each other.

"You came then," the woman said in a posh youthful voice.

"You summoned me, dear sister,"

"I did not summon you. It was a request,"

Cato cocked his head for a moment.

"Fine, I meant it as a request,"

"I would ask how you are but you asked me to this *place*,"

"We agree then? This is hardly a good place to eat,"

Cato felt a wave of confusion rush over him.

"I agree that this Bar looks posh but it doesn't feel right,"

"That's why we're here,"

Cato turned to her.

"I haven't seen you for years. Will we catch up? Or will you disappear again?"

"What do you mean again?"

"When father was forced to exile me for being gay. I wanted to say goodbye to you. You left the capital the morning before so I couldn't,"

"Cato, I'm sorry. I have always loved you. Saying bye was too hard. And I have some information you might find helpful,"

Cato was about to speak but his sister interrupted him.

"Help me now. Then I will give the information I have,"

"Fine, what do you want?

"See that man over there with the gold coin in his hat,"

A part of Cato wasn't in the mood, he just wanted to see his sister. He didn't want to be an errand boy for her.

Pushing the thoughts aside, Cato looked over to the far back of the Bar to see a lone man dressed in a fine shiny black silk suit with leather boots. Sitting at a small glass table with a few plates of finished food. Yet Cato had to admit the man wasn't bad looking. Was that why his sister was targeting him? Was Cato only here to be a wing man?

Then the comment about the gold coin made Cato's eyes narrow. Focusing on the hat, he couldn't see too much from this distance but it was a black top hat made from some strange material with a large gold coin in the centre.

The smell of freshly cooked seafood made Cato turn back to his sister to see her pinching a spiced piece of oyster from a passing waiter.

"Are you going to pay for that?" Cato whispered.

"I seem to remember you stealing your fair share of food from Father's kitchens,"

Cato smiled a little at the memories.

"That man over there. The coin in his hat. We need it,"

"Who's we?"

His sister looked around. Her eyes widened.

Looking over at the door to the Bar, three large men in blood Red and black armour walked in. Their hands on their sword hilts.

"Cato, please. Help me get the coin before they do and we will catch up,"

The sound of desperation and fear filled her voice.

Cato nodded.

He started to walk over to the man whilst his sister disappeared into the crowd.

As he passed vibrant colourful tables filled with fresh vegetables and culinary delights. Cato's nose was filled with immense smells of spices and flavours. His mouth tasted of so many great flavours. Maybe he would order some food after this. Whatever this is?

The sound of a chair moving made Cato look at the man. He was getting up and eyeing the three men in the black and red armour. His eyes were fearful.

Cato hurried over.

Screams filled the Bar.

Someone tackled Cato to the ground.

It wasn't his sister.

It was another man with a gold coin around his neck.

He punched Cato in the face.

More screams deafened the Bar.

Cato grabbed the man's neck. Snapping it.

The corpse fell.

Cato jumped up.

Whipping out his sword.

He spun around. The three men slaughtering the crowd.

Blood sprayed up the walls.

Bones crushed as swords shattered them.

People screamed as their heads were smashed.

Sweat dripped down Cato's back.

Where was his sister?

A man ran towards Cato.

He swung his sword. Bearing it in his chest.

The corpse fell to the floor. Revealing a tattoo.

A tattoo belonging to a Drug Gang.

That's why this place felt off. It was a drug den.

More screamed sliced through the air.

The three men in red and black armour stormed out.

Cato turned to them.

Everyone else was dead.

Piles of corpses laid at his feet.

Pools of blood covered the floor.

The men stared at Cato.

They saw the men Cato killed earlier. The gold coin around his neck.

The men stormed over.

Cato reacted. He didn't know why.

He charged over.

The men turned.

Cato whacked one of them with a powerful slash of his sword.

The armoured men met his blade.

They kicked him to the floor.

Cato felt the cold blood covered flood as his head hit it.

One man pointed his blade at Cato's throat.

He stared at the armoured face of the man. He didn't know what was happening. He didn't even know why he was here.

Warm blood covered his face.

The man dropped to the ground.

The other two men spun.

No one was there.

The men were distracted.

Cato forced himself up. Picked up his sword.

Metal whacking metal filled the Bar.

Cato looked to see his sister duelling with one of the knight men.

The last man charged at Cato.

He dodged out the way.

The man tripped.

His face smashing into the ground.

Cato thrusted his sword into his back. Bones and metal cracked as the sword chomped through the flesh.

Turning to see his sister standing over another corpse, Cato really wanted to shout and scream at her. What the hell was this? Who were these people? What was his sister involved in? So many questions, so little time.

His sister picked up the gold coin from around the man's neck and she admired it in her hands.

All Cato wanted to do was leave and be done with this. Just to see what would happen Cato started to walk towards the door. And of course trying to ignore the sound of bones being crushed under his feet as he walked.

"What are you going, Catoian? I need you,"

He stopped and slowly turned around.

"No, you didn't need me. You needed a blade. Has it really been that long that you've forgotten how to be a sister? I was still healing when you called. Be grateful I'm able to fight. Be grateful… be grateful you have a brother who loves you,"

Cato walked away.

When he got to the door, placing his blood covered fingers on the cold door handle, he felt his sister come over to him.

"I am sorry. Please stay. Help me finish this. I need you. You're the only person I can trust,"

***

After reluctantly agreeing to help his sister to end whatever this was, she had led Cato to… Cato didn't know. As he looked around all that surrounded him were strange black painted walls that supported a broken and slightly burnt thatch roof. The tiny box room was a building all in itself.

Cato had no idea why his sister bought him here but he didn't care for the bitter, burnt ash that floated in the air. Making it smell like a burnt forest and his mouth tasted of charred flesh.

It was just typical of his sister to bring him to the location of another incident. All Cato wanted to do was to get to know his sister once again. It wasn't his fault he was exiled for his own protection.

The sound of children's footsteps splashing in the mud outside reminded Cato of when him and his sister would run around outside together as children. Playing it and all sorts of other games.

Yet this only reminded Cato that it was always the same. Whenever his sister needed him, he was there. From the time a dragon had coughed and shot out fire at her to the time she was a teenager and attacked by bandits. He was always her protector. And she was his.

That unfortunate truth made Cato pull all his doubts and anger towards her away. He loved his sister.

However, Cato did miss his dragon Pendra. He would love to have stroked her long smooth shiny scales about now, and it would be pretty great to have someone to talk to.

A part of Cato was confused about why his dragon asked to remain with the beautiful Caden and his dragon, Kadien. Yet Cato knew why in part. He suspected his dragon might have a thing for Kadien. They were both beautiful and stunning dragons but...

The opening and slamming of a wooden door behind him made Cato turn around to see his sister walk in. Wearing her long shiny metallic blue cloak that highlighted her eyes and youthful face. The smell of her posh, expensive perfume made Cato cover his mouth quickly until he could get used to the smell. Had she really had time to freshen up?

"Where have you been?" Cato asked.

"Tracking?"

"Tracking what?"

"Our target,"

"Sister, speak fully or I will walk away,"

His sister paused.

"Why do you want the coin? We have the man's coin from his neck. Why are you still hunting the hat man?"

She turned to face him.

"Cato, I presume you know I've been working for the delivery investigators or whatever that unpronounceable word is,"

"Yes,"

"Four months ago, we found a number of our delivery dragons had been brainwashed or had their minds wiped to make them deliver… classified stuff,"

"*Classified*. I am the Prince,"

She rolled her eyes.

"Fine, you know the drug Catico?"

His eyes widened.

"Of course. That drug can wipe the minds of men and women. Turning them into mindless drones after three months of taking it. There's no known cure. Don't those people fall under the control of a Witch Priest?"

His sister slowly nodded.

"Yes, the drug was being transported all over our Father's Realm. We intercepted the majority of the drug but we do not know who was behind it,"

"Until now?"

"Correct, we learnt the identity of the suppliers a few moments before news of your return from father reached me,"

"The Coin,"

"Yes, Catoian they are called Dragon Coins. The network uses them as identification, and we know where they're meeting. We just needed a coin or two to gain entry,"

Cato walked around her a few times before he stopped.

"The hat man, he is important?"

She nodded.

"But why were those other men attacking him?"

She took a deep breath.

"We managed to read a letter from a drug gang member to an unknown someone. I think there was some doubt to hat man's loyalty. We think someone wanted to kill him,"

"But you want to kill him to attack the network?"

"Yes, Cato. It seems the drug gang still trusts him, and he seems to be a powerful member. Killing him would greatly damage the network of the drug gang. Which is why we are here,"

Cato walked in front of her and stared her dead in the eye.

"What have you done?"

"This is one of their drug houses. They will come here to store the drugs. We will kill them,"

"The hat man?"

"He always comes here,"

The temperature shot up.

Sweat dripped down Cato's face and back.

He looked up.

The thatch was burning.

Massive yellow and red flames engulfed the roof.

Black smoke filled the box room.

Their eyes watered. Their vision a blur.

They both dashed outside. Their swords raised.

The thick mud splashed up their legs.

Their vision cleared.

Cato's eyes narrowed.

Three strong women dressed in thick red and black armour stood there with ugly box-like helmets.

Each holding a long black sword in each hand.

Another figure stood in the middle.

The man wore pure black knight armour wearing a hat with a golden coin sewed into it.

He had to be the hat man.

The women charged.

Lashing and slashing their swords as they went.

Cato dodged.

He kicked mud into their faces.

Their helmets protected them.

They swung once again.

Cato back flipped away.

He saw the hat man rush over to his sister.

He had to help them.

The women slashed at Cato's leather armour.

He tried to block them.

Three blades slashed at his chest.

Slicing into his leather armour.

The women stormed towards him with powerful swings.

Cato kept jumping back.

He wanted to strike.
There wasn't an opening.
He looked to his sister.
She was being beaten up by the man.
Cato needed to help her.
He couldn't let another bully attack her.
Cato jumped towards the women.
The move caught them off guard.
Cato thrusted his sword into one of their throats.
Rivers of blood gushed out.
Cato picked up one of the corpse's sword.
The other two women were distracted.
Cato whacked one with his swords.
Shattering her jaw.
She tried to scream.
Cato whacked her again.
She fell to the floor in agony.
The last women swung at Cato.
He jumped out the way.
Making the woman's sword slam into her friend on the floor.
Blood squirted into the air.
The last woman stumbled back.
Maybe in horror.
Cato didn't care.
He slashed her throat.
She landed with a thud.
For good measure, Cato smashed his boot down on her head.
It cracked like an egg. Shattering her skull.
Cato turned to his sister.
She was on the ground.
Her armour covered in thick mud.
The hat man stood over her. His sword high.

Cato stormed over. Tackling the hat man to the ground.

He slammed his fists into the man's face.

The man's nose cracked.

Cato felt a strong hand grab his neck.

He hesitated.

The hand threw him onto the ground.

Cold mud seeped into Cato's leather armour.

Fists rapidly punched Cato's face. His face was knocked around.

He couldn't see.

Everything was a blur.

He could feel his brain moving inside him.

These fists kept slamming into him.

Cato felt his nose bleed.

His jaw bone aching.

Something was about to snap.

The fists moved to his throat.

Cato gagged as the two massive hands tightened around his throat.

He grabbed at the hat man's hands. Cato pulled. It was useless.

The man's face smiled in twisted delight.

Cato went lightheaded.

A blade slashed the man's head off.

Blood squirted into Cato's eyes.

He screamed in shock.

Two hands pulled him onto his side.

Cato took long deep breaths as his lightheadedness went. He constantly wiped his watery eyes to get the blood out of them.

Despite his eyes watering so badly, he couldn't even see. He knew it was his sister's muddy hands stroking his back to comfort him.

After a few minutes, Cato's eyes cleared, and he opened them properly to see the chopped off head of the hat man in front of him. Including the gold coin in the hat.

Cato stopped for a moment to actually think about what was happening. His sister, the Princess, was hunting a drug gang but for some reason he was the only person she could trust. Why?

Also, why was she investigating the drugs? Cato knew he had been in exile for a few years but that didn't change the fact that his Father had thousands of intelligence officers and police spread throughout the Realm. They could and would investigate this matter. Something didn't sit right.

The smell of his sister's posh, expensive perfume made his attention turn to the hat. His sister's long elegant fingers were stretching towards it.

Cato grabbed it.

"What!" his sister screamed.

Cato swirled around in the cold mud to look down at her who was also sitting in the mud.

"The truth. Why are you investigating? Why am I the only person you can trust? I have a team. Two dragons and... basically a boyfriend. They could have helped,"

His sister looked at him and smiled.

"Caden,"

Just the sound of his name made Cato smile.

"Yes. You know Father sent him to me to save him from being executed for discovering about the Witch Cults,"

"I do know. I was the one who persuaded Father to send him to you. We both agreed you two would like each other,"

Cato wanted to thank her, but this felt like her avoiding the question.

"Why am I the only person you can trust?"

She paused.

"You know the Witch Cults. Radical groups of extreme witches and wizards who want to… I do not know. Their threat is growing. These drugs I think are another plan of theirs',"

"Flood the Realm with the drug. Get the people to become mind dead and their slaves,"

"Exactly. This is planning on another level. Especially for them,"

"My question,"

"Yes, Catoian. Delivery dragons are extremely well protected. Their settlements, food, water is protected almost as well as Father is. The dragons know not to eat anything else. They know how important they are to the Realm,"

"So, you think the delivery dragons who had their minds wiped were drugged?"

"I do,"

"An inside job?"

"Yes, Cato. I believe there is a group inside the Royal Delivery Service that is working for the Witch Cults. I have reported to Father. We both agree this is a massive threat to the Realm but… there are so many Witch Cult threats to deal with. That's even before we consider the threats from the Orks in the North and the creatures and trolls in the south,"

Cato took a step back for a moment. There was so much happening in the Realm. The orks, the trolls and creatures, the Witch Cults and his personal mission against the Warden of Faith who was stopping him from re-joining the Royal Family.

The thought of the noose tightening around his country made him sick. Cato needed to act but he knew he needed his team. He needed Pendra, Kadien but most of all he needed Caden. That beautiful boy with his stunning longish blond hair.

Cato knew he had been away too long but at least he had a good story to tell them when he returned. Then he remembered something about his sister wanting to tell give him some information.

"What information were you going to give me?"

Her eyes looked to the ground for a moment for rising back up to meet his.

"I know you are looking for the Warden of Faith. He has arrived back in the Capital, and he is staying with the Grand Cardinal in the Great Cathedral,"

Cato smiled for a moment. He now knew where the Warden of Faith was. The foul, disgusting fanatic that was holding his Father to the ancient laws of The Royal Code. With this fanatic dead, he could rejoin his family and be with the stunning Caden. That's all he really wanted.

Looking at the hat, Cato got his sword and sliced off the gold coin. Passing it to his sister.

"We both have our own missions but let's worry about them tomorrow. I think I saw a tavern a few blocks away. Shall we?"

His sister nodded and hugged him. Cato beamed a little. Knowing he was finally going to catch up with his sister.

GET YOUR FREE AND EXCLUSIVE SHORT STORY NOW! LEARN ABOUT NEMESIO'S PAST!

https://www.subscribepage.com/fireheart

About the author:

Connor Whiteley is the author of over 60 books in the sci-fi fantasy, nonfiction psychology and books for writer's genre and he is a Human Branding Speaker and Consultant.

He is a passionate warhammer 40,000 reader, psychology student and author.

Who narrates his own audiobooks and he hosts The Psychology World Podcast.

All whilst studying Psychology at the University of Kent, England.

Also, he was a former Explorer Scout where he gave a speech to the Maltese President in August 2018 and he attended Prince Charles' 70th Birthday Party at Buckingham Palace in May 2018.

Plus, he is a self-confessed coffee lover!

OTHER SHORT STORIES BY CONNOR WHITELEY

Blade of The Emperor
Arbiter's Truth
The Bloodied Rose
Asmodia's Wrath
Heart of A Killer
Emissary of Blood
Computation of Battle
Old One's Wrath
Puppets and Masters
Ship of Plague
Interrogation
Edge of Failure
One Way Choice
Acceptable Losses
Balance of Power
Good Idea At The Time
Escape Plan
Escape In The Hesitation
Inspiration In Need
Singing Warriors
Dragon Coins
Dragon Tea
Dragon Rider
Knowledge is Power
Killer of Polluters
Climate of Death
Sacrifice of the Soul
Heart of The Flesheater

Heart of The Regent
Heart of The Standing
Feline of The Lost
Heart of The Story
The Family Mailing Affair
Defining Criminality
The Martian Affair
A Cheating Affair
The Little Café Affair
Mountain of Death
Prisoner's Fight
Claws of Death
Bitter Air
Honey Hunt
Blade On A Train
City of Fire
Awaiting Death
Poison In The Candy Cane
Christmas Innocence
You Better Watch Out
Christmas Theft
Trouble In Christmas
Smell of The Lake
Problem In A Car
Theft, Past and Team

Other books by Connor Whiteley:

The Fireheart Fantasy Series
Heart of Fire
Heart of Lies
Heart of Prophecy
Heart of Bones
Heart of Fate

City of Assassins (Urban Fantasy)
City of Death
City of Marytrs
City of Pleasure
City of Pleasure

Agents of The Emperor
Return of The Ancient Ones
Vigilance
Angels of Fire

The Garro Series- Fantasy/Sci-fi
GARRO: GALAXY'S END
GARRO: RISE OF THE ORDER
GARRO: END TIMES
GARRO: SHORT STORIES
GARRO: COLLECTION
GARRO: HERESY
GARRO: FAITHLESS
GARRO: DESTROYER OF WORLDS
GARRO: COLLECTIONS BOOK 4-6

GARRO: MISTRESS OF BLOOD
GARRO: BEACON OF HOPE
GARRO: END OF DAYS

<u>Winter Series- Fantasy Trilogy Books</u>
WINTER'S COMING
WINTER'S HUNT
WINTER'S REVENGE
WINTER'S DISSENSION

<u>Miscellaneous:</u>
RETURN
FREEDOM
SALVATION

www.ingramcontent.com/pod-product-compliance
Lightning Source LLC
LaVergne TN
LVHW020508080526
838202LV00057B/6230